STICK LIKE GLUE

COLIN WELLS

WEST GEORGIA REGIONAL LIBRARY SYSTEM
Neva Lomason Memorial Library

Artesian Press
P.O. Box 355 Buena Park, CA 90621

Take Ten Books
Mystery

Other Take Ten Themes:
Chillers
Sports
Adventure
Disaster
Thrillers
Fantasy

Project Editor: Liz Parker
Cover/Text Illustrator: Fujiko Miller
Cover Designer: Tony Amaro
©2001 Artesian Press

 *Artesian* **Press**

ISBN 1-58659-004-9

Chapter 1

The man was huge, practically a giant. In the flickering red and blue light his face shone with sweat. He moved slowly towards the window, reaching for the desk. He stood by the desk for a moment, then parted the curtains above it. The colored lights grew brighter, showing his eyes. They were the eyes of a trapped animal. The man looked down at the desk, then at the bed beside it, where the boy lay awake. His hands, gripping the curtain, slowly let it go. Large hands, strong-looking, reaching down to the boy in the bed...

The marble trick didn't work anymore. Bummer, thought Sam Tanaka. He hesitated, then knocked instead. "Ronald?" he called. "Yeah. Come in," his older brother answered after a moment. Sam opened the door and the marble rolled free. It had been an old game of theirs: Sam would fire a small marble under the door to announce his arrival. It always got a laugh from Ronald—the sound of the marble rolling along the wood floor, then bouncing off the legs of the desk by the window. He had wanted to use it to welcome his brother home—after four years—but the marble stuck with a soft *thud* under the door.

"Hey," Sam said gently. Ronald must have been asleep. His face was red, the black hair above his forehead wet with sweat. He looked up from the chair.

"Marble woke you up, huh? I'm not surprised it didn't work, it's been a long time." Sam sat down on the bed, moving Ronald's crutches to one side. They were the kind with braces for your arm, rather than pads for your shoulder to rest on. Ronald needed them to walk, and even then he moved only with difficulty. Most of the time he was pushed around in the wheelchair.

"Yes," Ronald said after a short pause.

"Welcome home, anyway," Sam said.

"Welcome home yourself." Sam blinked in surprise; it was not like Ronald to say something like that. "How was camp?" Ronald added.

"Same as always, okay." Actually, camp was great. This summer Sam had taught archery, canoeing, and swimming. As usual, though, he didn't discuss his athletic activities with his brother.

Sam had been adopted as an infant. So while the rest of the Tanakas were short with very dark hair, Sam was large, muscular, and had very blond hair. "Mom says it's time to go."

To celebrate Ronald's return, their parents had planned a special dinner at his favorite Italian restaurant. For four years, he had lived at Stillbrook, a special "home" for mentally retarded children. Ronald had been born with cerebral palsy, a condition that made it hard for him to control his muscles. His movements were weak and awkward, his voice slurred. It had taken the doctors a long time to realize that, like most children with cerebral palsy, Ronald was not mentally retarded at all. The condition that made him different affected only his body, not his mind.

Right now, his mind seemed worried about something.

"You sure you're okay?"

"Yeah. I guess I fell asleep. I'm just trying to remember ..." Ronald paused.

"What?"

"Nothing, I guess. Let's go."

Sam pushed the wheelchair out of the room.

They were beginning dessert at the restaurant when Mr. Tanaka was called to the phone. He returned in a hurry. "All right, let's go, guys, June. There's some trouble at the house." He paid the bill and they left quickly.

Sam noticed the red and blue flashing lights before they got to the house. He glanced at his brother. Ronald was staring straight ahead. As they got closer, Sam could see that the lights were coming from two police cars sitting in front of the house. Mr. Tanaka parked in the driveway.

As Sam was unfolding the wheelchair, a policeman came along the pathway that led behind the house. Sam knew him: Officer Pete Matthews of the Simmsville Police Department. The small town did not have a large police force. Matthews had helped arrest a burglar at the Tanaka house four years earlier.

"Evening, Mr. Tanaka, Mrs. Tanaka," said the policeman. "Our radio dispatcher told me they'd got you in the middle of dinner. We had a report of a prowler from Mr. Meeks, across the street. He saw a flashlight moving in this room here." Matthews pointed to a dark window beside the front door. "He also knew where you were, luckily,"

"That's Ronald's room," Mrs. Tanaka said. She sounded both puzzled and worried. Ronald settled into the chair.

Matthews said, "I've got a man at the back door. That door looks like it was forced. I haven't gone in yet, but no one's getting out through the back."

Sam noticed that the policeman had his hand on the pistol in his holster.

Just then another car pulled up behind the police cars. The brown four-door had the words *Simmsville Register* painted in large white letters on the side. A big man with a brown handlebar mustache got out.

He walked quickly up the front walk. He greeted the group, saying he had heard the report of the break-in on his police radio. He turned to Ronald. "Hey, how's my buddy?" he asked, ruffling the boy's hair. Sam guessed that this was Joe Streller, the reporter who had written a recent news story about Ronald.

Matthews, leaving the front door locked, disappeared around the back. A few minutes later, he opened the front door, unlocking it from within. "No sign of the prowler," he reported. "But I'm afraid there's been some vandalism. You'd better come inside and make sure nothing is missing."

As they went in, Mrs. Tanaka gasped, "Oh, no! Look at this mess." Pictures were crooked, two lamps knocked over, and books all over the floor. Most of the furniture lay on its side. The torn-up remains of the room's cushions formed a pile in the middle of the carpet. Several photograph frames had been taken apart, and the parts were scattered. In the kitchen, light fixtures had been smashed and several squares of tile ripped up from the floor.

Chapter 2

The clean-up went quickly. "No real damage," said Officer Matthews, careful not to get his own fingerprints on anything. "It's often a lot worse, this kind of vandalism. As a matter of fact, I'd say you were pretty lucky." The other policeman had gone.

"Maybe you interrupted whoever it was, Pete," suggested the reporter.

"Could be," Matthews said. "We got here pretty quickly. I was on patrol in the neighborhood." Matthews turned to Mr. Tanaka. "Right now, I think I should question your neighbor before it gets too late." Mr. Tanaka nodded and led the policeman to the door.

Joe Streller stayed longer, chatting

with the boys and their parents in the living room. He introduced himself to Sam.

"The football player, right? You were away at camp while your brother was playing Sherlock Holmes at Stillbrook. You missed all the action. When did you get home?"

"Today," Sam answered. "Mom and Dad sent me your article, though. It was good." Streller seemed like a nice guy. Better than Matthews, who acted kind of cocky with that big gun on his belt.

"Well, I had a good subject. Your brother really surprised them all." Ronald looked embarrassed, so Streller changed the subject. "Anyway, it doesn't look like there's a story here, luckily." He said goodnight and left.

Sam went up to his room to get ready for bed. He grabbed his guitar off the bed for a few minutes of fun before brushing his teeth. A folded piece of paper slipped out from under the instrument's strings. He unfolded it. It was a drawing with the heavy lines of a felt-tip pen. Sam drew in his breath sharply. "Oh, wow."

He ran down to Ronald's room.

"Check this out," he said, handing his brother the drawing. "It was folded up in the strings of my guitar."

The cartoon-like drawing showed a car disappearing down a road, with little puffs of smoke coming out of the tailpipe and up from the wheels. A stick-figure boy lay sprawled in the road. Next to the boy was a football helmet and a guitar, both cracked in two jagged pieces. Tire tracks ran across the boy's middle, and a dark shadow of blood oozed from his head. His eyes were two X's. At the bottom were the words, "Tell anyone, and this is you."

The phone rang in the living room. Knowing their parents had gone to bed, Sam stepped out to answer it.

"Hello?"

"Samuel Tanaka?" The voice was unfamiliar, an older man's.

"Yes."

"You don't know me, but here's what's gonna happen." The voice was kind of rough, as if the man had a bad cold. "In a few seconds, you're gonna say yes again, like you just did. After that, you're not gonna say anything. You're just gonna listen. Because if you don't something very bad might happen to you or your family. Something very, very bad. Like maybe a serious case of death. No joke. You understand? Here's where you say yes, kid."

Sam let his breath through his teeth in a low hiss. "Yes," he whispered.

"Good. I can tell you, I've been waiting for you and your brother to get home. Since I saw in the paper about him being such a genius, and coming home to live. I guess the name Johnson means something to you."

It did. Four years earlier, a man named Johnson had stolen a valuable stamp collection started by Sam's grandfather. Officer Matthews had helped arrest Johnson. "The guy who paid you a little visit a few years ago," the man with the scratchy voice continued. "You remember his famous helper? Well, you're talking to him. Or, he's talking to you." The man chuckled.

Although Johnson was caught near the house with the stamp album, the most valuable eight stamps had been removed from the leather book. Johnson later told the police that he had passed them to someone else. Neither the helper nor the eight stamps had ever turned up.

"Here's the deal. Johnson was in your brother's room, right?" Ronald had awoke and, in the light of the night-light by his bed, seen Johnson before the burglar fled out the back door. "Johnson went in there to look out the

13

window when the cops got there.

"Well, he never passed me no stamps. He hid 'em—hid 'em when he saw the cops closing in. And your brother saw where. Or he saw something that would tell him where. As long as everyone thought your brother was retarded, no problem. But as soon as he got unretarded, big problem.

"That's where you come in. Since I couldn't find them tonight, you and your brother are gonna find them for me. Sorry to interrupt your nice little dinner, but I'll interrupt more than that if I don't get what I want.

"And you won't say a word about this to anyone. If you do," said the man who seemed to have a cold but didn't cough or blow his nose, "someone's gonna get hurt for nothing. Did you get my little message? If not, check your guitar. If you open your mouth, someone dies. It's that simple. On the other hand, do what I say, kid, and everyone will be okay. Understand?"

"Yes."

"Good. Find those stamps. I'll be in touch." There was a click as the caller put the phone down.

Chapter 3

Slowly, Sam replaced his own receiver. Two thoughts were in his mind. One was that the stamps had been hidden in their house the whole time. Close behind this idea came the memory of the man's threats.

He went back into Ronald's room. Ronald sat in the same position by the bed. The two brothers looked at each other for a moment.

Sam was fourteen, younger than Ronald by two and a half years. He had always believed in his older brother. With Sam, Ronald wasn't nearly as shy and quiet as he was around others, even their parents. As much as anything, Ronald's silence had made the doctors think he was retarded. Sam had visited Ronald at Stillbrook and had seen how his brother was treated as an object, just a thing to be washed and fed.

Then Ronald started finding stuff: a pair of glasses carelessly misplaced, a pack of cards. And finally he found Dr. Gantz's big gold wristwatch. Joe Streller's article told the story of the lost watch. For two days, Ronald took any opportunity to quiz the busy doctor. The doctor finally remembered splashing some sticky liquid on his hands the day before. He didn't recall taking the watch off, or even washing his hands. Ronald studied the layout of the two washrooms near the doctor's office, then asked an attendant to look in the garbage dumpster outside. The watch had slipped from the shelf above the sink into the wastebasket, falling noiselessly among crumpled paper towels. The basket had been emptied into the dumpster, where the watch was found, still among the paper towels. A few hours after that, a garbage truck emptied the dumpster.

Within a week, Ronald was packing to come home, and Joe Streller was writing his article. The article told how surprised the doctors had been when Ronald found the watch. A boy who they thought was mentally retarded had solved a mystery that had defeated them! Dr. Gantz, who was in charge of Stillbrook, was impressed at how Ronald had found a way to show his intelligence. "That boy loves a good mystery," the doctor said. "He obviously doesn't belong here."

Now it looked as though Ronald's reputation for finding things might have gotten them in trouble. "The guy who drew this just called me," Sam said, fingering the piece of paper.

Ronald nodded.

Ronald listened in silence as Sam

told him about the one-sided conversation. He continued to sit there, thinking, for a few minutes after Sam finished.

"I don't understand why he left the drawing for you, if I'm supposed to know where the stamps are," Ronald said.

Sam shrugged. "Do you remember anything?" he asked. "Do you know where they are?"

"I'm not sure," came the reply. "I don't think so."

Sam didn't understand how you could be unsure whether you knew something. You either knew or your didn't. He was getting frustrated. He wished his friend Susana was there; she always understood what Ronald meant when he said things like that.

He made a small movement, and Ronald spoke. "He was positive that Johnson hid the stamps somewhere, but he didn't know where. He just thought they were somewhere I would know?"

"Right. He must have figured they were somewhere in your room, like when Johnson came in here. Or somewhere around it. But it's been four years. And all your stuff was moved out. How could they not have been found? I think he's bluffing, or just fooling around." But he didn't really.

"Did he say whether he'd talked to Johnson?"

Sam thought. "No, he didn't."

"Hmm." Ronald rocked back and forth in the chair. Sam knew that meant he was thinking. "And he said he was sorry he'd interrupted our dinner?"

"Well, yeah, but I don't think he really meant it."

Ronald said, "Right," but sounded unsure.

"So what do we do?" Sam asked, trying to get things straight.

"We do what we're supposed to do," Ronald grinned. "We find the stamps. Tomorrow."

Yes, Sam thought, it was time to call Susana.

Chapter 4

"Okay, come and get it," said Susana Cruz, although Ronald and Sam were already sitting at the kitchen table. She put down plates piled with scrambled eggs, fried potatoes with onion, bacon, and toasted bagels. Her eyes twinkled; Susana loved to cook, and she loved to eat even more.

It was the next morning, and the three of them had the house to themselves.

"So, what's all the mystery about?" she asked, spreading a mountain of cream cheese on a bagel.

Sam produced the drawing and put it on the table so that she could see it. He heard her catch her breath, just as he had. "Jeez. What sicko drew that?" She bit into her bagel and chewed.

As they ate, Sam told her about the break-in and once again repeated what the man with the scratchy voice had told him. "Wow. He actually said that? 'A serious case of death!' Come on! It sounds like a bad movie. So Johnson's story about passing the stamps was a lie, huh? Cool. I guess you didn't really see anything, though," she said to Ronald. "I mean, that's obvious, or you would have the stamps."

Ronald continued to eat silently. "But they thought you were mentally retarded," the girl said. "Retarded guys don't know what they're seeing. So Johnson's friend is suddenly worried that you're smart and will remember something. That doesn't explain why he never tried to recover those stamps before."

Ronald chewed. She looked at him with a smile. "Okay, so tell us."

Ronald said, "I don't think he knew they were hidden."

Susana thought about this. "I don't get it."

As always, Ronald spoke slowly. "I don't think Johnson told him where he hid the stamps. I'd say Johnson didn't trust his friend very much."

"Call him X," Sam suggested.

Susana laughed. "Just like a movie again. Anyway, what makes you think that?"

Ronald said, "The fact that X didn't look for the stamps a long time ago."

"How do you know X could even talk to Johnson?" Susana asked. "Johnson was in prison, right? The cops would look for anyone who got in touch with him."

"This might be wrong, but I think the two must have talked after Joe's article. Johnson told X about hiding the stamps, but he still wouldn't say where."

"What's the point of that?" Susana demanded, helping herself to another piece of bacon.

"If I'm right," Ronald said, "Johnson told him to see if I remembered anything. And I don't. X realized that meant the stamps may be hidden in the house."

"I get it. I think," said Susana. "What you're saying is Johnson read the article, got nervous about you, talked to X, and told him just enough but not too much. Right? So X could try to scare us."

Smiling, Ronald said, "Right."

"Johnson couldn't tell X everything, because Johnson was afraid X might take the stamps."

"Right again," Ronald said.

"So what happens if we find the stamps? Wait, I know. He hopes we're scared enough to give them to him."

"And he's right," Sam said, only half joking. He laid his knife and fork neatly on his plate and shrugged. "Ronald thinks we should find the stamps. But maybe we should, um, tell someone about this."

"No way. We find the stamps, dummy." Susana grinned. "Just like you say, Ronald. After we've got them, we tell Mr. Mafia Hit-Man to take a long walk off a short dock. Then we get police protection or something. Hire a bodyguard." She stopped grinning as the drawing on the table caught her eye. "Well, maybe not. But don't worry, we'll think of something."

"Find the stamps first." Ronald said.

"Right. So say we find them. Then what?" Sam wasn't going to give up. After all, he was the one who had talked to "Mr. Mafia Hit-Man."

"Then we have what he wants."

"I know that—" Sam began. Susana interrupted him.

"Yeah! Of course!" she exclaimed. "We'll have him right where we want him. Tell him to come and get it—and we'll knock him out and tie him up." She nudged his wheelchair playfully. "Yeah, good plan. Sucker him in, and nail him!"

"So I guess Ronald and I can start looking, while you clean up," she said, hitting Sam on the arm.

Chapter 5

They looked. They looked in Ronald's closet, under his rug, and behind his radiator. They looked in the base of the lamp and under the cushions of the armchair. Then they turned the armchair over and checked the bottom of it. They examined the bottoms of the desk drawers and the back of the desk, in case the stamps had been taped there. Susana went through the drawers. "Look at this stuff," she exclaimed. "I guess your mom left it all here. Glue, scissors, old pieces of construction paper, string, a pencil, a bunch of crayons, marbles."

"Yeah, my mom used to have me work with that stuff. I wasn't very good with scissors," Ronald said.

The search continued. They felt along the top of the window, and then along the ledge at the top of the door frame. They then took the bed apart and examined the frame and the box spring. They stirred up dustballs and found an old sock. They did not find the stamps.

As they were about to give up on searching the room, Ronald went to the window and examined the hem of the curtain. He exclaimed in surprise, and the other two rushed over. "What's up? Found something?"

"I don't know. Look here," Ronald said.

They felt along the bottom of the hem. "Hey, what's this? It's torn!" said Susana. "No, it's cut. The whole thing is slit along the bottom!"

She and Ronald looked at each other. "Yeah." She nodded. "That must be when old Rollo saw the lights.

Someone was looking here for the stamps."

After lunch, they continued the search outside Ronald's room.

Susana went home at about six o'clock, grumbling in disgust. Mr. and Mrs. Tanaka came home soon afterwards. At supper, the boys were quiet. Susana came back later, looking cool and refreshed after a shower. The three met in Ronald's room.

"I say we call the cops and tell them everything," Sam declared. "What's wrong with that?"

"For a football jock, you can be pretty gutless," Susana said. "What are the cops going to do? They can't find the guy. And they can't protect anyone if the guy is serious about getting nasty. We should do it ourselves."

"Do what?" Sam cried in frustration. "The only thing we can do is hope he doesn't get angry that we didn't find the stamps. There's nothing else we can do without them."

He looked at Susana. "Right? Am I right?" he asked.

The girl shrugged. "I don't know. There's got to be something we can do."

"There is," Ronald said. He paused.

"What?" they both demanded.

Ronald spoke quietly but firmly. "We don't need the stamps to trap him."

There was a pause as Sam and Susana thought it over. Then Susana said, "Yeah, you're right. Of course. All we have to do is tell him we've got them. He won't know the difference."

"Oh, sure!" Sam exclaimed. "Then he sees there aren't any stamps, and who does he pick for lunch meat? Me, that's who! Not a chance. Not unless we call the cops and have them catch the guy."

"Okay, wimp." Susana was disgusted. "We'll call the cops so they can hold your hand. We'll call that nice Officer Matthews. Give him a chance to get the big promotion. Right?" She looked at Ronald.

"Yes," Ronald agreed. "That's exactly what we do. We'll see if the police can catch X when he comes for the stamps. Now we just have to wait for him to call."

Chapter 6

Two days later, the phone call finally came. X gave Sam simple directions.

"Put the stamps in an envelope, and tape the envelope inside a newspaper. At exactly noon tomorrow, go to the alley behind Mason's Drug Mart, in the center of town. There's a trash can by a telephone pole, the only telephone pole in the alley. Put the newspaper in the trash can, and leave. That's all. Remember—come alone and leave right away, without looking around or looking back."

Sam told Ronald, then phoned Pete Matthews. The policeman had agreed to help them trap the caller. Pete had mentioned the plan to his friend Streller, who saw a chance for a good story. The plan called for the two of them to arrest the man as he picked up the stamps—or what he thought were the stamps. Streller decided to bring a camera and a video camera.

At a few minutes before noon the next day, Ronald and Susana watched as Sam folded a piece of paper into an envelope, then taped the envelope into a copy of the *Simmsville Register*. He then zipped the newspaper securely into his school backpack. "All set," he said.

"Remember, don't look around. Especially not for Joe or Officer Matthews." The two adults had been in position since nine-thirty that morning. "Be careful."

Sam got on his bike, waved at Ronald, and set off on the short trip to the center of town. The pack was light and snug against his back. It was a nice day, not too hot. He hoped Streller and Matthews were keeping out of sight.

He turned down the alley. There was the telephone pole, with the trash can next to it. He coasted to a stop and removed his pack. He got the newspaper out and dropped it gently in the trash can. Simple. He zipped the pack back up and put it on. Then, keeping his eyes straight ahead, he rode off down the alley and turned towards home.

Susana and Ronald were waiting as he pulled up. "How did it go?" Susana asked.

"No problem. Now all he has to do is show up."

"He will if he wants those stamps badly enough," said Susana.

Ronald said, "Well, all we can do now is wait for Joe to call."

Joe Streller had figured that the caller would come by about one o'clock. He thought the man would watch Sam arrive, then make sure that no one had followed him. Streller and Matthews were hidden in buildings at either end of the alley. They were in positions to watch the trash can and to block off the alley at both ends.

Three o'clock came and went. By four-thirty, Sam and Susana had grown restless. By six, they were ready to ride their bikes into town to see what had gone wrong.

Ronald, however, seemed to become quieter. When Streller finally called at about six-twenty, he perked up for a moment. But the news that no one had appeared at the trash can sent him back into a deep silence.

"Well, that stinks," Susana complained. "What do we do now?"

"I don't understand," Sam said. "How could he know that we didn't find the stamps? Do you think he realized we told Joe and Pete about him? I mean, great. Now he comes after me."

"He knows we told," Ronald said. "But he won't come after you."

"Huh? What do you mean?"

"I think he knew that if we found them we wouldn't turn them over to him. We'd give them to our parents, or to someone we trust."

"I don't get it," Sam said.

"But that's not why he didn't show up," Ronald continued. "Remember how the guy on the phone said he was sorry for interrupting our dinner?"

"Yeah." Sam sounded puzzled.

"I noticed that Pete Matthews said the police radio person mentioned calling us back from the restaurant."

"Yeah, he did," Sam agreed. "Wait a minute—"

"Aha," Susana interrupted, "so that's why you didn't want the police to help catch him. Only someone with a police radio would know you were called back home in the middle of dinner. And the caller knew, so he must have had a police radio. You suspected the cops, huh? But what made you trust Pete? Okay, so he's a nice guy after all, but we didn't know that then."

Ronald said, "I didn't trust him. I still don't."

After a moment, Susana said quietly, "You'd better tell us what's going on."

Ronald shifted in his chair. "Sam said at the beginning he thought the guy on the phone was bluffing. He also said the guy sounded like he had a cold, you know, scratchy voice. And you said he sounded like a bad movie."

"You think it was an act? Maybe he was disguising his voice?" Susana asked. Ronald nodded. "And he would only do that if he was afraid we—or Sam—would recognize it," she said slowly. "Pete, huh?"

Ronald nodded. "Remember, he helped arrest Johnson? But Joe Streller also has a police radio. And he knew about the stamps from that article he wrote about Granddad, remember?"

The article had come out shortly before the stamps were taken. Just after that Ronald had gone to Stillbrook. "None of this is for sure. I just thought it was most likely one of them. They always seem to be around. If someone else picked up the paper, I was wrong. If no one picked it up, that's because X was one of the people we asked to watch for him. I didn't want to be right. I like them both."

"It might even *be* both of them, working together," Susana said.

"Oh, great!" Sam burst out. "What, do we ask them? We'll never know, will we? Anyway, those stamps are probably miles away from here. This whole thing is so stupid! We don't know anything for sure. We don't know who called, we don't know who broke in, and there's no way to find out. If it is Joe or Pete, they're going to be ready for any trap we try. We can't pretend we've suddenly found the stamps now. They'd never believe us."

"No," agreed Susana. "If we told them we had them, they'd want to see them."

"Great," Sam repeated. "We're stuck."

There was a short silence. Susana watched Ronald, now sitting comfortably in his chair. She smiled, a small smile at first, then larger. "Hey," she said to Sam. "I think your brother has another plan."

"I do," Ronald said. "I think I know how to trap whoever made those calls."

"How?" asked Sam.

"Well," Ronald said slowly, "we think it's Joe or Pete, right? What if we made them both think that Johnson has told someone else where the stamps are. Someone he trusts. If either Joe or Pete is X, he will try to get them from the new guy. We can get a policeman to play the new guy and pretend to break into our house."

"You think X would really try that?" asked Susana.

"I think he will do anything to get the stamps. He's too proud to admit defeat."

"Especially by a kid who was supposedly retarded," said Susana. Ronald nodded. "And that's why you want to defeat him, isn't it?" The older boy was silent. "It's like a contest, isn't it?"

"Maybe," Ronald said. "I guess I'm proud, too."

Chapter 7

As the door closed softly behind them, Sam looked once more at the sign on it: Chief Takao Ohara. Had they forgotten anything? He didn't think so. He and Susana started down the hallway to the police station's front entrance. It was early afternoon four days later, and they had one more stop: the offices of the *Simmsville Register*. However, they were not quite finished at the police station.

Pete Matthews was on duty at the front desk. "Hey, you guys, how's it going?" Matthews looked surprised to see them. "Uh, any word from our friend?"

"Yeah, sort of," said Susana. "Well,

not word, we haven't heard from him. Actually, we're not sure it's him at all."

"But we figure it must be. Or at least, Ronald figures," Sam said.

"I'm afraid you've lost me."

Susana said, "X. We've seen him!"

"Huh? Where? When?"

"He's been watching our house," Sam said. "We're sure of it. The same brown car has either been parked on the street or driving by slowly. Ronald thinks it's X, and that he's going to try something soon. Since the day he was supposed to show up at the trash can, we keep seeing the car. The third day, yesterday, he parked across the street for a long time."

"You should have said something about this to me." Matthews was grim.

"We didn't want to bother you any more, after last time," Susana said, looking embarrassed.

Sam said, "He hasn't been around so far today, and Ronald thinks he'll break in tonight. We told Dad what was going on, but he said that the phone calls were a prank and that we were imagining things about the car. So we came to see Chief Ohara. The chief was a friend of Granddad's, and they were Granddad's stamps. We figured he might listen to us."

"He said he doesn't have enough policemen to waste on such a small chance," Susana said bitterly. "He thought it was a prank, too, because no one showed up at the trash can to get the stamps."

Matthews said, "I still don't understand that. There's no way he could have known we were there. I'll have a talk with the chief. Sounds like there ought to be someone watching your house at night for a little while."

Sam and Susana exchanged a glance. Sam said, "Thanks. Right now we're going to see what Joe Streller has to say."

That night, a light breeze rustled in the leaves of the trees. Cool air came in through the open window of the upstairs hallway. Sam, Ronald, their parents, and Susana were gathered around the window, Ronald in his chair, the rest standing over him to watch the yard.

The big house was quiet and snug, floodlights shining on the front and sides. Only the back remained dark. The group waited patiently. An occasional whispered comment failed to disturb the silence.

At around one-twenty A.M. Sam checked his watch. It seemed to become even quieter. A few minutes later, a shadow moved silently towards the house. As it passed through some light, they could see the shape of a man, and the dark covering of a ski mask over his head and face.

The man disappeared from view as

he reached the house, almost directly beneath them. A few moments went by, then came a muffled *crack*, followed by the faint tinkling sound of small pieces of glass falling onto a hard surface. More time passed.

Without warning, the man reappeared and retraced his silent journey. As he returned to the shadows, something moved out to stop him—a second figure. The newcomer raised his arm. Moonlight shone off something dark and metallic in his hand. They both stood there, frozen.

Suddenly, a ring of powerful lights snapped on. The two figures stood clearly lit in a circle of harsh white light. At the same time, a voice shattered the long silence. "This is the police. You are surrounded. Drop the gun and lie down on your stomach with your arms out to the side!" Two uniformed policemen ran up to the second figure, now lying on the ground. One, crouching, held a gun while the other handcuffed the man's hands behind his back.

The policeman then hauled the handcuffed man to his feet. Sam recognized the handcuffed man as Joe Streller. The masked man stayed still. Then, as if he'd forgotten all about it, he stripped off the ski mask. It was Pete Matthews. Matthews watched coldly as Streller was led away.

Chapter 8

"I must say, you certainly made a convincing burglar, for an officer of the law," Mrs. Tanaka said the next evening. "Can I tempt you with another slice of pie, Pete?"

"Yes, ma'am! Thank you indeed. It's fine pie, and that was a fine dinner, too."

"Mmm, very good pie," agreed Susana, eyeing it hopefully.

"Well, I'm glad we didn't have to wait up more than once." Without asking, she served Susana a second piece.

"I have a question, Ronald," said Pete Matthews through a mouthful of pie. "Why were you so sure X was bluffing?"

"Yeah," agreed Sam. "Since it was my neck on the chopping block, my guts on the line, my—"

"Samuel Tanaka, you are at the dinner table."

Ronald said, "Your neck—exactly. The note came to you, and the phone calls. He never threatened me, although I was the one who supposedly knew what he wanted to know."

Pete looked puzzled.

"I don't get it," Susana said.

Ronald continued. "It just made me think that maybe X was someone who knew me."

Pete nodded. Ronald continued, "Sam and Susana both noticed that the phone calls sounded like an act. It seemed likely the threats were, too."

"Then there were the two articles, one just before the stamps were stolen, and one just before the break-in," Susana pointed out. "Joe was trying to make it seem that the guys who broke in got the idea from his article. It threw suspicion away from him."

"It sure did," Matthews agreed. "When all along, Streller hired Johnson to do the break-in, using information he'd collected while working on the article about your grandfather. It was a good article, too." The article had told the story of Toshio Tanaka, who had immigrated to California from Japan and Hawaii in the 1920s.

"Anyway, Joe stayed in touch with Johnson," Matthews continued. "We found records of visits he made to Johnson in prison, the last one just after you got home, Ronald. They must have planned to recover the stamps together, after Johnson got out. When they could watch each other."

Ronald said, "They didn't trust each other."

"With good reason," Pete said. "Each of them wanted the stamps for himself. But they were both stuck without them—Johnson because he was in prison, Joe because he didn't know where they were."

"And Johnson refused to tell him," Sam added.

"That's why your plan was so good, because they didn't trust each other. Inventing a guy in a brown car made Joe think that Johnson had found someone else, someone he trusted to return the stamps to him. Joe had to catch the guy in the act if he wanted to take the stamps from him. I thought Johnson had found someone, too, until Chief Ohara told me the truth." Pete laughed. "So you thought I was a crook!"

"Ronald knew that if you were innocent, you'd go to the chief," said Susana.

"Well, most likely." Ronald smiled.

"So it looks like Joe wrote the article about Ronald just to get closer to him," Susana said with disgust. "So he could find out what he knew. What a weasel."

"And after all this," Sam said, "we still haven't found those stupid stamps."

"So what is my genius brother going to do about school, Mom?" Sam asked, drying a dessert plate. He and his mom were alone in the kitchen.

"The doctors say we can get private tutoring," said Mrs. Tanaka, pausing for a moment at the sink. "It's so good to have him back."

"I think he feels that way, too. Have you noticed how much more he's talking?"

"Yes, I have." She smiled. "You two still stick together, don't you?"

"Like glue, Mom."

"That's good. I'm proud of both of you." She gave him a quick hug.

On his way to Ronald's room, Sam paused to pick up a marble from the ashtray beside the phone. He smiled.

The marbles, left over from a childhood game, seemed to keep turning up. He knelt by Ronald's door and fired the marble. It stuck with the same dull *thud* as before.

Thud. Suddenly, everything fell into place in Sam's head. Johnson by the window, standing over the desk. The night light, right by the bed, which would let him see the stuff on the desk: glue, scraps of construction paper, scissors.

Even the timing was right. Ronald had gone away just after the burglary. Other than the day he got home from camp, Sam hadn't tried the marble trick for the four years his brother was away.

He opened the door, and the marble rolled free. Ronald had turned his chair, a slow grin spreading across his face. Susana, in the armchair, seemed puzzled. Sam knelt again and peered through the gap between the floor and the bottom of the door. He stuck a finger under the door and felt paper. Susana whispered, "I don't believe it. The stamps were glued underneath the door the whole time. *That's* why the marble wouldn't go through."

Very carefully, Sam pulled the narrow strip of glued and folded paper away from the bottom of the door and brought it over to the desk. He laid it on the desk. Ronald handed him a pair of scissors. "You'd better do it," Ronald said. "As I said, I'm not so good with scissors."